This Faber book
belongs to:

➤ A FABER PICTURE BOOK ◄

Jennyanydots

The Old Gumbie Cat

Written by T. S. Eliot

Illustrated by

Arthur Robins

FABER & FABER

I have a Gumbie Cat in mind,
   her name is Jennyanydots;
Her coat is of the tabby kind,
   with tiger stripes and leopard spots.

All day she sits upon the stair
or on the steps or on the mat:

She sits and sits and sits and sits—
    and that's what makes a Gumbie Cat!

But when the day's hustle and bustle is done,

Then the Gumbie Cat's work is but hardly begun.

And when all the family's in bed and asleep,

She slips down the stairs
to the basement to creep.

She is deeply concerned with the ways of the mice—

Their behaviour's not good and their manners not nice;

So when she has got them lined up on the matting,

She teaches them music,

crocheting and tatting.

I have a Gumbie Cat in mind, her name is
    Jennyanydots;
Her equal would be hard to find, she likes
    the warm and sunny spots.

All day she sits beside the hearth
   or in the sun or on my hat:
She sits and sits and sits and sits—
   and that's what makes a Gumbie Cat!

But when the day's hustle and bustle is done,

Then the Gumbie Cat's work is
but hardly begun.

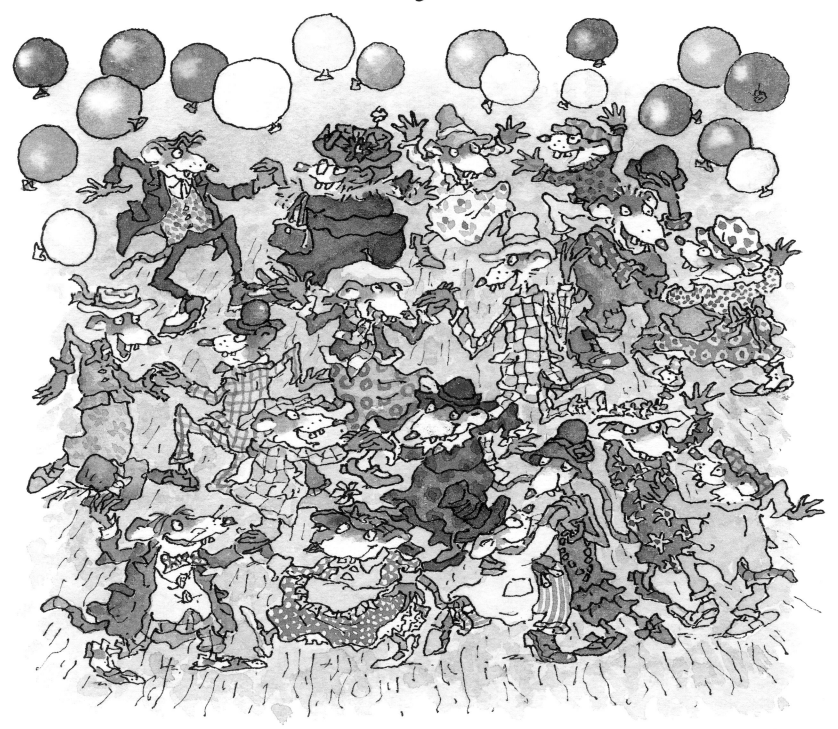

But when the day's hustle and bustle is done,
Then the Gumbie Cat's work is but hardly begun.

She thinks that the cockroaches just need employment
To prevent them from idle and wanton destroyment.

So she's formed, from that lot of disorderly louts,
A troop of well-disciplined helpful boy-scouts,

With a purpose in life and a good deed to do—
And she's even created a Beetles' Tattoo.

So for Old Gumbie Cats let us now give three cheers—

On whom well-ordered households depend,
  it appears.

From the original collection,
'respectfully dedicated to those friends who have assisted its
composition by their encouragement, criticism and suggestions:
and in particular to Mr T. E. Faber, Miss Alison Tandy,
Miss Susan Wolcott, Miss Susanna Morley, and the Man in White Spats. O.P.'

First published in 1939 in Old Possum's Book of Practical Cats by Faber and Faber Ltd, Bloomsbury House, 74—77 Great Russell Street, London WC1B 3DA
This edition first published in the UK in 2020
This edition first published in the US in 2020

Printed in Italy

A CIP record for this book is available from the British Library
ISBN 978—0—571—35280—7

2 4 6 8 10 9 7 5 3 1